P9-DDP-576

Parables in action

Dog Paws and Sandy Claws

By Susan Titus Osborn
Illustrated by Ronda Krum

With love for my cousin Laura.
May you learn more about Jesus
through reading this book.

Parables in Action Series

Lost and Found
Hidden Treasure
Comet Campout
Moon Rocks and Dinosaur Bones
Cooks, Cakes, and Chocolate Shakes
The Super-Duper Seed Surprise
Flip-Flop Fishing
Dog Paws and Sandy Claws

Published by Concordia Publishing House
3558 S. Jefferson Avenue, St. Louis, MO 63118-3968
Manufactured in the United States of America

Library of Congress Cataloging-in-Publication Data

Osborn, Susan Titus, 1944-
Dog paws and sandy claws / by Susan Titus Osborn.
p. cm. — (Parables in action series)
Summary: Suzie and her friends demonstrate helpfulness and caring when they rescue an injured dog and take it to the veterinarian. Includes a retelling of Jesus' parable about the good Samaritan.
ISBN 0–570–07140–2
[1. Conduct of life—Fiction. 2. Christian life—Fiction. 3. Dogs—Fiction. 4. Parables.] I. Title.
PZ7.07975 Do 2001
[Fic]—dc21
00-010073

---

1 2 3 4 5 6 7 8 9 10 10 09 08 07 06 05 04 03 02 01

Hi! My name
is Suzie. I'm waiting
after school for my friends.
We will walk home together.

Here they come now.

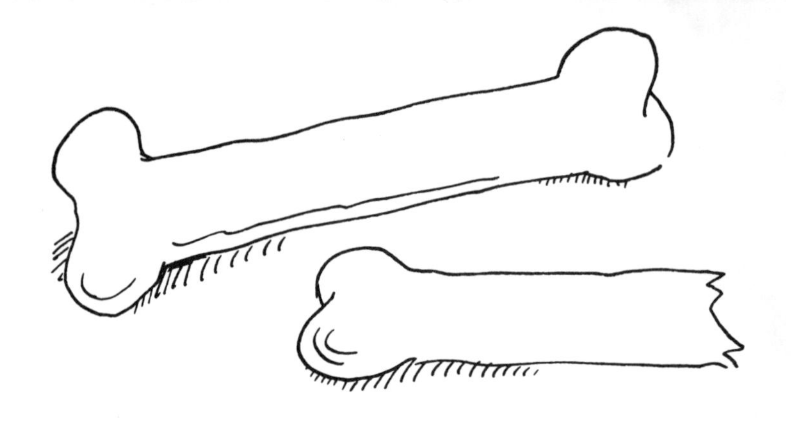

"Hi, Mario. What's in the sack? Are those your dinosaur bones?" I asked.

"Yes, Suzie," he said. "I'm taking them home. They are so special. I can't leave them at school."

Mario owns a field. He found the dinosaur bones buried there. He gave some to the museum. Today he brought four of them to school for Show and Tell.

The Spy walked beside Mario. He wrote notes in his spy book. The Spy was always writing notes in his spy book. Today he shared his recipe for chocolate milk shakes during Show and Tell.

One day we baked a cake. It was for Mr. Zinger's birthday. Mr. Zinger is our teacher. We also made chocolate milk shakes. Both recipes were in The Spy's book. The cake and the shakes were yummy!

Bubbles walked up. She was dressed in a chef's apron. She wore a tall chef's hat. "Here. Do you want a cupcake?" she asked.

Mario and I said, "Sure." Bubbles handed out cupcakes for Show and Tell. They were yummy!

The Spy stuck his finger into his cupcake. He said, “Zook! Zook!” He licked his finger.

I knew what he said. I’d been friends with The Spy for a long time. “Zook! Zook!” was his secret code for “yummy.” The Spy liked to talk in secret code.

"You are a good cook, Bubbles," I said.

Bubbles smiled. "Thanks. I'm practicing for my latest TV ad. It's for Mandy's Baking-Is-Fun Oven."

Bubbles was always practicing for her TV ads. One time I saw her picture on a jar of bubbles at the store. We all called her "Bubbles" after that. Her real name is Nan.

Just then Mr. Zinger drove by. He stopped and waved. "Good-bye, Susan. Thanks for sharing your pictures. They were great for Show and Tell. I want to put them on the board. May I borrow them?"

"Sure you can," I said.

"Good-bye, Mario," said Mr. Zinger. "The kids liked your dinosaur bones. Did they come from your empty lot?"

"Yes, they did," Mario said.

"Your cupcakes were yummy, Nan. And so were your milk shakes, Larry. See you on Monday, kids." Mr. Zinger always calls us by our real names. The Spy's name is Larry.

Mr. Zinger drove away. Bubbles waved a pancake turner at him. We all waved goodbye. Mr. Zinger is the greatest!

We walked home. Bubbles pretended to flip pancakes. She threw them up into the air. Then she caught them. The Spy wrote more spy notes.

Suddenly we heard a noise. It sounded like an animal crying. We looked in the bushes. A dog was lying there. His paw was stuck in a big trap. He looked so sad.

“Look! His paw is bleeding!” I shouted. I said a quick prayer. I asked Jesus to help us help the dog.

Mario held the trap with both hands. He carefully opened the jaws. The Spy bent down. He pulled the dog’s paw out.

Bubbles looked at the dog. “I think I’ve seen that dog before,” she said. She bent over. She looked at his tag. “His name is Sandy Claws.”

“I’ve never seen him before,” I said.

"I don't think Sandy lives around here," said Mario. "We'd better take him to a vet. I'll run home and get my wagon."

"That's a good idea," I said.

Mario raced down the street. He lived nearby.

A man in a business suit came by. I waved to him. "Sir, could you help us?" I asked. "This dog is hurt."

He looked at me. He looked at Sandy. Then he looked away. He walked on by. He pretended that he didn't hear me.

Sandy cried. I patted his head. "It will be all right, Sandy. We'll take care of you."

Then Mrs. Miller came by. I knew she would help.

"Mrs. Miller, could you help us?" I asked. "This dog has a hurt paw."

"Oh, dear," said Mrs. Miller. "I'm late for the beauty shop. I need my hair done. I need my nails done. I don't have time to stop." She walked on by.

I looked at Sandy. His paw was really bleeding now. I said another prayer. I asked Jesus to help us help Sandy.

Suddenly I had an idea. "Bubbles, I'm going to make a bandage. Can I use your apron?" I asked.

"That's a good idea, Suzie," said Bubbles. She took off her apron. She handed it to me.

I folded it over. I put it around Sandy's paw. Around and around it went. I tied it tightly.

"That should stop the bleeding," I said.

Sandy barked. "WOOF!" I think he agreed with us.

Then another dog barked. "WOOF! WOOF! WOOF!" It was Mario's dog, Woof. Mario was back with his wagon. Woof ran beside him.

Woof saw Sandy. He ran over to him. He rubbed noses with Sandy. They became friends.

We lifted Sandy. We put him into the wagon. We were very careful. We didn't want to hurt Sandy's paw.

There was a blanket in the wagon. Sandy curled up on the blanket. He closed his eyes. He felt safe.

Mario said, "Doctor Brown is around the corner. He's Woof's vet. Let's take Sandy there."

Mario pulled the wagon. I pushed from behind. The Spy wrote notes in his spy book. Bubbles walked in circles. She flipped her pretend pancakes in the air. Woof ran beside the wagon. He wagged his tail and barked. "WOOF!"

Mario pulled the wagon into Doctor Brown's office. A nurse sat behind a desk. She asked, "May I help you?"

"Yes," said Mario. "We found a dog in the bushes. He hurt his paw. It's bleeding."

The nurse walked over to Sandy. She looked at his paw. She frowned. “I’ll tell Doctor Brown right away,” she said. She left the room.

A few minutes later she came back. “Doctor Brown will see you now,” she said. “Follow me.” She walked down a hall. She opened a door.

Mario pulled Sandy into a little room. Bubbles, The Spy, and I came too. Woof had to stay outside.

The vet put Sandy on his table. He looked at Sandy's paw. "This dog is going to need stitches," he said. "I will sew up his paw. It will cost $50."

We looked at one another. We didn't have $50!

"I'll pay for it, Doctor Brown. Put it on Woof's bill," said Mario. "I'll sell some more dinosaur bones to the museum. We'll raise the money."

Doctor Brown nodded. He sewed up Sandy's paw. He was very careful. Sandy wasn't crying. He looked happy now. The vet put Sandy in the wagon. We pulled him back to Mario's house.

Sandy limped into the house. He curled up on the rug. Woof curled up next to him. They touched noses again. They were really good friends now.

Mario turned on the TV. We watched the news. A man said, "A famous dog is missing. His name is Sandy Claws. If you find him, please call the TV station."

Mario called the TV station. He said, "We found your missing dog. He has a hurt paw. We took him to the vet. Now he's much better."

Soon there was a knock at the door. It was the nice man on TV. He walked into Mario's house. He smiled at Sandy. He patted his head. "I'm glad to see you, Sandy," the man said.

Sandy barked. "WOOF! WOOF! WOOF!" Sandy was glad to see the man too.

"Thank you for finding our lost dog. We were doing a TV ad. Sandy must have walked away. We were so busy. We didn't see him go," the man said.

"Bubbles does TV ads," I said.

Bubbles turned around. She flipped her pretend pancakes one more time up into the air.

"I'm practicing for my latest TV ad. It's for Mandy's Baking-Is-Fun Oven." Bubbles smiled at the man.

"Would you like to do an ad with Sandy?" he asked.

"That would be fun," said Bubbles.

“I need four kids for a new ad,” said the man. “Could you teach your friends to act? Then they could do a TV ad too.”

“Sure,” said Bubbles. “I’ve done lots of ads.”

“WOW! We get to be on TV,” said Mario.

"Just like Bubbles," shouted The Spy. He was so excited. He forgot to talk in secret code.

I hugged Bubbles. "This will be so much fun," I said. "I've never been on TV before!"

The man smiled. “Now is your big break,” he said.

Woof wagged his tail. He barked. “WOOF! WOOF! WOOF!”

Sandy barked too. “WOOF! WOOF! WOOF!”

“Sandy agrees with us,” said the man.

We all laughed.

The Parable of the Good Samaritan

Based on Luke 10:25–37

One day Jesus told a parable:

A man was going from Jerusalem to Jericho. Some robbers beat him and ran away.

A priest came along. He walked on by.

Another important man called a Levite came along. He walked on by too.

Then a Samaritan came along. He bandaged the man's wounds. He put the man on his own donkey. He took him to an inn. He took care of the hurt man.

Suzie, Mario, Bubbles, and The Spy found Sandy on the way home from school. They bandaged his hurt paw. They put him into a wagon. They took him to the vet. They took care of the hurt dog.

Jesus says, "Love your neighbor as yourself." Jesus loves us and He helps us to show love to one another. We show His love when we help others who are hurting.

Hi, everyone!
Jesus wants us to take care of one another. He wants us to help others when they are hurting. Here's one way you can put Jesus' Parable of the Good Samaritan into ACTION!

Parables In Action

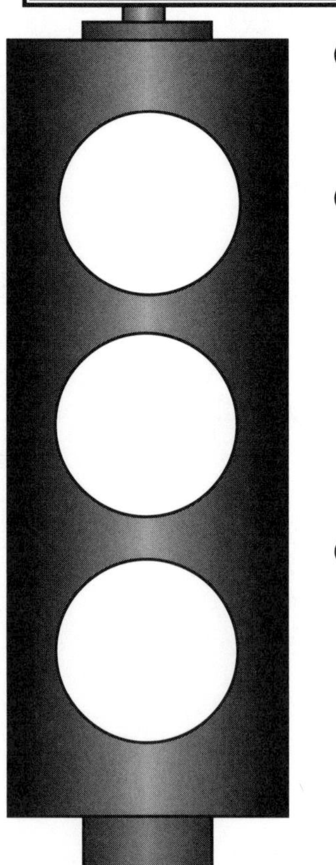

Get Ready. Find some colored construction paper, scissors, glue, colorful markers, and glitter.

Get Set. Fold the paper into quarters so it looks like a greeting card. Draw a picture on the front with the markers. Use the glue and glitter to make it sparkle. Write "Get Well" and "Jesus Loves You" on the inside.

Go! Have your mom or teacher take you to a home for older people. Give the card to someone in the home or hospital who doesn't have many friends. Tell that person about Jesus and the Parable of the Good Samaritan.

3041